TOP 5

JESS CASTLE

Big mouth

5 WORDS THAT DESCRIBE YOU

1

2

3

4

5

5 WORDS OTHER PEOPLE WOULD USE TO DESCRIBE YOU

1

2

3

4

5

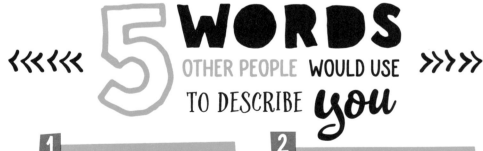

5 CHARACTER TRAITS YOU ADMIRE

1

2

3

4

5

1

2

3

4

5

5 CHARACTER TRAITS THAT ARE OVERRATED

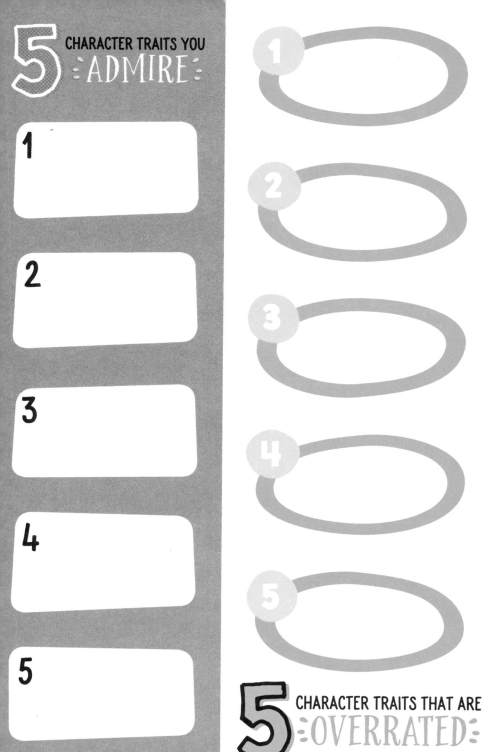

5 PEOPLE

WHOSE EXAMPLE YOU FOLLOW

1 ....

2 ....

3 ....

4 ....

5 ....

5

RULES TO LIVE YOUR LIFE BY

1 ______________________________

2 ______________________________

3 ______________________________

4 ______________________________

5 ______________________________

5 ANTIHEROES

1 ....

2 ....

3 ....

4 ....

5 ....

5 WORDS

PEOPLE USE TOO MUCH

1 ------------------------

2 ------------------------

3 ------------------------

4 ------------------------

5 ------------------------

5 worst WAYS TO BREAK UP

1

2

3

4

5

1

2

3

4

5

5 best WAYS TO MAKE UP

5 THINGS YOU SHOULD NEVER DO VIA TEXT

-
-
-
-
-

5 WORDS YOU SHOULD NEVER USE ON YOUR PROFILE

-
-
-
-
-

5 BEST MOVIES *of all time*

1 ____________________

2 ____________________

3 ____________________

4 ____________________

5 ____________________

5 FOODS THAT SHOULD BE BANNED FROM THE *movies*

1

2

3

4

5

5 WORST PLACES FOR A DATE

-
-
-
-
-

5 BEST PLACES for a FIRST DATE

1.
2.
3.
4.
5.

5 songs THAT WILL STAY ON YOUR PLAYLIST FOREVER

1

2

3

4

5

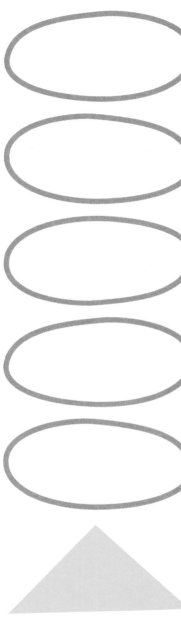

5 MOST annoyingly CATCHY SONGS

5 SONGS you know ALL THE WORDS TO

1

2

3

4

5

5 artists YOU WOULD SWAP LIVES WITH

1

2

3

4

5

5 MOST USEFUL INVENTIONS

1

2

3

4

5

5 MOST DANGEROUS INVENTIONS

1

2

3

4

5

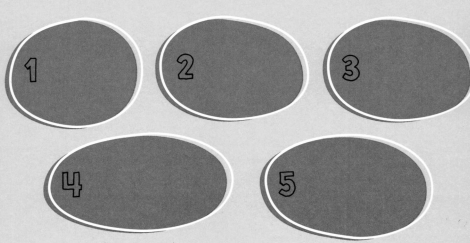

5 MOST IMPORTANT HISTORICAL FIGURES

1

2

3

4

5

1

2

3

4

5

5 THINGS YOU'D LOVE TO BE FAMOUS FOR

5 FAMOUS PEOPLE (LIVING) YOU'D LOVE TO MEET

1 ....

2 ....

3 ....

4 ....

5 ....

5 FAMOUS PEOPLE (NOT LIVING) YOU'D LOVE TO MEET

1 ______________________________

2 ______________________________

3 ______________________________

4 ______________________________

5 ______________________________

5 THINGS YOU WOULD DO IF YOU WERE A MILLIONAIRE

1 ....

2 ....

3 ....

4 ....

5 ....

5 THINGS

YOU WOULDN'T DO FOR ANY AMOUNT OF MONEY

1 ------------------------

2 ------------------------

3 ------------------------

4 ------------------------

5 ------------------------

5 most MORTIFYING MOMENTS

1

2

3

4

5

5 PROUDEST MOMENTS

1

2

3

4

5

5 CHANCES YOU SHOULD HAVE TAKEN

•

•

•

•

•

5 RISKS THAT WERE SO WORTH TAKING

★

★

★

★

★

5 THINGS THAT NEED TO BE *invented*

1 ____________________

2 ____________________

3 ____________________

4 ____________________

5 ____________________

5 THINGS EVERY HOME *should have*

1

2

3

4

5

5 SOCIAL MEDIA POSITIVES

-
-
-
-
-

5 SOCIAL MEDIA NEGATIVES

1.
2.
3.
4.
5.

5 ways CATS are better than DOGS

1

2

3

4

5

5 WAYS DOGS are better than CATS

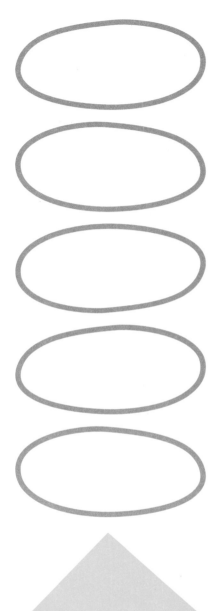

5 REASONS to have a PET

1

2

3

4

5

5 animals HUMANS CAN LEARN FROM

1

2

3

4

5

YOUR 5 WORST HABITS

1

2

3

4

5

5 WORST HABITS IN OTHER PEOPLE

1

2

3

4

5

5 NAMES YOU'D BE HAPPY TO HAVE

1

2

3

4

5

1

2

3

4

5

5 NAMES YOU'RE GLAD YOU WEREN'T GIVEN

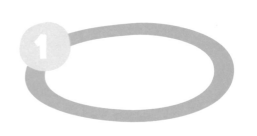

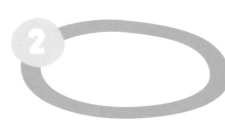

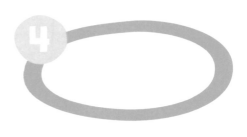

5 THINGS

PEOPLE SHOULD NEVER DO ON A TRAIN

1. ....
2. ....
3. ....
4. ....
5. ....

5 THINGS EVERYONE SHOULD DO ONCE

1. ______
2. ______
3. ______
4. ______
5. ______

5 THINGS YOU WILL NEVER REGRET

1 ....

2 ....

3 ....

4 ....

5 ....

5 THINGS YOU MIGHT REGRET

1 --------------------------

2 --------------------------

3 --------------------------

4 --------------------------

5 --------------------------

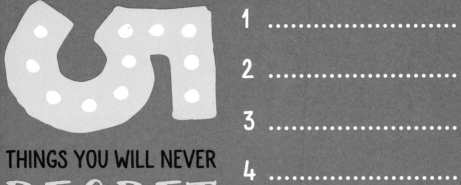

5 classic SHOWS YOU'D RERUN

1

2

3

4

5

1

2

3

4

5

5 classic SHOWS YOU'D REBOOT

5 REALITY SHOWS YOU'D HAPPILY APPEAR ON

-
-
-
-
-

5 REALITY SHOWS YOU'D NEVER >>> APPEAR ON <<<

-
-
-
-
-

5 PEOPLE YOU'D SHARE A TENT *with*

1 ______

2 ______

3 ______

4 ______

5 ______

5 PEOPLE YOU'D HAPPILY BE STRANDED ON A *desert island* WITH

1

2

3

4

5

5

WORST PEOPLE TO BE TRAPPED IN AN ELEVATOR WITH

-
-
-
-
-

5 PEOPLE YOU'D START A BUSINESS WITH

1.
2.
3.
4.
5.

5 drinks YOU COULDN'T LIVE WITHOUT

1

2

3

4

5

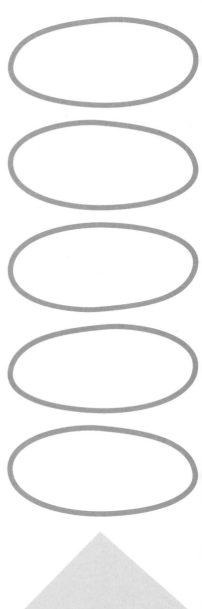

5 BEST MEALS you've ever >>> HAD <<<

5 THINGS you would only eat IF YOUR LIFE DEPENDED ON IT

1 ______

2 ______

3 ______

4 ______

5 ______

5 THINGS YOU *wouldn't eat* IF YOUR LIFE DEPENDED ON IT

1

2

3

4

5

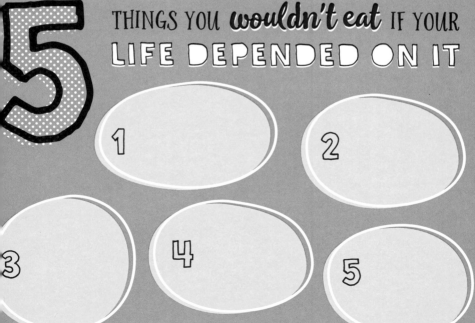

5 SONGS THAT ALWAYS MAKE YOU HAPPY

1

2

3

4

5

5 SONGS THAT ALWAYS MAKE YOU SAD

1

2

3

4

5

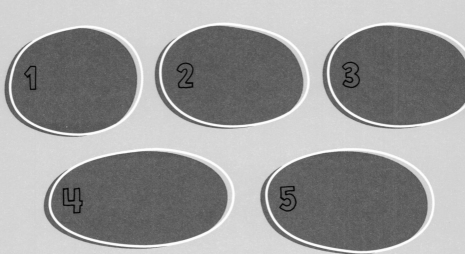

5 WORST MUSIC VIDEOS

1

2

3

4

5

1

2

3

4

5

5 CREEPIEST SONGS

5 RULES

YOU HAVE BROKEN

1. ....
2. ....
3. ....
4. ....
5. ....

5 TIMES WHEN THEFT CAN BE JUSTIFIED

1. ______________________
2. ______________________
3. ______________________
4. ______________________
5. ______________________

5 LAWS YOU WOULD PASS

1 ....

2 ....

3 ....

4 ....

5 ....

5 LAWS YOU WOULD REPEAL

1 ---------------------------

2 ---------------------------

3 ---------------------------

4 ---------------------------

5 ---------------------------

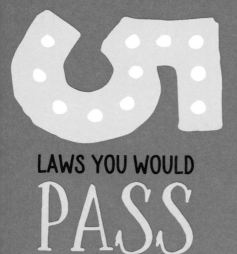

5 dream VACATION DESTINATIONS

1

2

3

4

5

1

2

3

4

5

5 worst VACATION DESTINATIONS

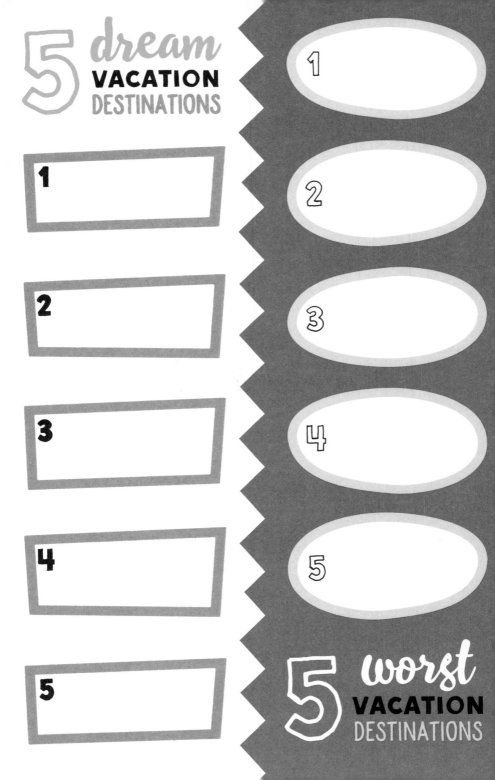

5 REASONS TO VISIT AN AMUSEMENT PARK

-
-
-
-
-

5 REASONS TO NEVER VISIT AN AMUSEMENT PARK

-
-
-
-
-

5 THINGS YOU LOVE ABOUT YOUR town

1 ______________________

2 ______________________

3 ______________________

4 ______________________

5 ______________________

5 THINGS YOU DON'T love about your town

1

2

3

4

5

5

NAMES THAT WOULD SUIT YOUR TOWN BETTER

- ....
- ....
- ....
- ....
- ....

5 BEST PLACES TO EAT

1. ....
2. ....
3. ....
4. ....
5. ....

5 worst FOODS

1

2

3

4

5

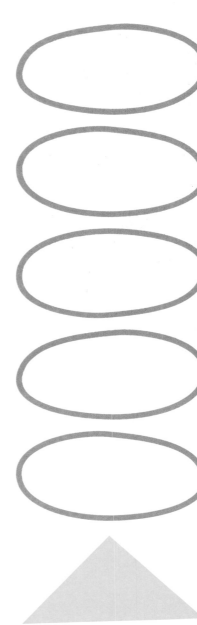

5 CELEBRATION FOODS that are OVERRATED

5 FOODS that taste better DEEP FRIED

1

2

3

4

5

5 best ever CANDY BARS

1

2

3

4

5

5 BEST SMELLS

1

2

3

4

5

5 WORST SMELLS

1

2

3

4

5

5 BEST FLAVORS

1

2

3

4

5

1

2

3

4

5

5 WORST FLAVORS

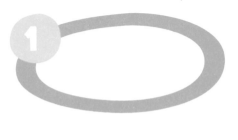

5 THINGS

THAT PUT YOU IN A GOOD MOOD

1 . . . .

2 . . . .

3 . . . .

4 . . . .

5 . . . .

5 THINGS THAT PUT YOU IN A BAD MOOD

1 ______________________

2 ______________________

3 ______________________

4 ______________________

5 ______________________

5 THINGS YOU FEAR

1 ....

2 ....

3 ....

4 ....

5 ....

5 THINGS YOU WISH FOR

1 ---------------------------

2 ---------------------------

3 ---------------------------

4 ---------------------------

5 ---------------------------

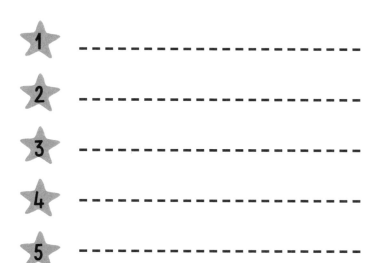

5 funniest PEOPLE (DEAD OR ALIVE)

1

2

3

4

5

1

2

3

4

5

5 best SINGERS (DEAD OR ALIVE)

5 DISNEY CHARACTERS WHO'D BE REALLY IRRITATING IN REAL LIFE

5 DISNEY CHARACTERS YOU'D DATE IN REAL LIFE

5 THINGS YOU *would do* IF YOU COULD FLY

1 ____________________

2 ____________________

3 ____________________

4 ____________________

5 ____________________

5 THINGS YOU WOULD DO *if you could see through* WALLS

1

2

3

4

5

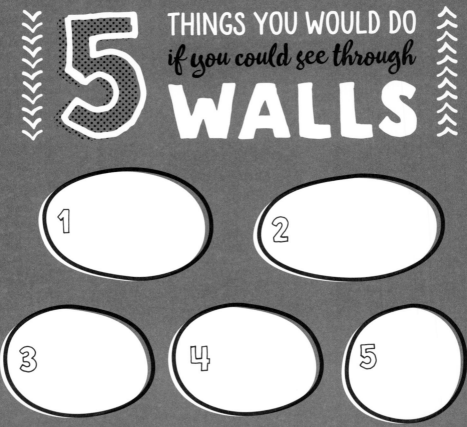

5

THINGS YOU WOULD DO IF YOU COULD READ MINDS

-
-
-
-
-

5 THINGS YOU WOULD DO *if nobody* COULD FIND OUT

1.
2.
3.
4.
5.

5 classes YOU WISH YOU STUDIED HARDER IN

1

2

3

4

5

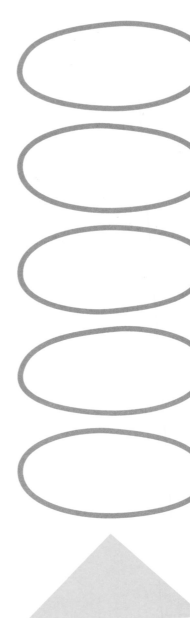

5 CLASSES you wish you'd TAKEN

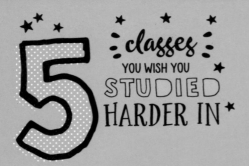

5 CRAZES that are STUPIDER THAN PLANKING

1 ____________________

2 ____________________

3 ____________________

4 ____________________

5 ____________________

5 crazes THAT ARE DUE A REVIVAL

1

2

3

4

5

5 REASONS WHY THE FUTURE IS BRIGHT

1

2

3

4

5

5 INVENTIONS THAT CHANGED THE WORLD

1

2

3

4

5

5 GADGETS THAT WILL BE REDUNDANT IN 20 YEARS' TIME

1

2

3

4

5

1

2

3

4

5

5 JOBS THAT WILL NOT EXIST IN 20 YEARS' TIME

5 SPORTS YOU LOVE TO PLAY

1 ....

2 ....

3 ....

4 ....

5 ....

5 SPORTS YOU PREFER TO WATCH

1 ______________________________

2 ______________________________

3 ______________________________

4 ______________________________

5 ______________________________

5 SPORTING RULES YOU'D CHANGE

1 ....

2 ....

3 ....

4 ....

5 ....

5 GREATEST SPORTS PEOPLE OF ALL TIME

1 ------------------------

2 ------------------------

3 ------------------------

4 ------------------------

5 ------------------------

5 FICTIONAL CHARACTERS YOU IDENTIFY WITH

1

2

3

4

5

1

2

3

4

5

5 FICTIONAL CHARACTERS YOU'D MARRY

5 FICTIONAL PLACES YOU'D CHOOSE TO LIVE IN

-
-
-
-
-

5 BEST BOOKS

-
-
-
-
-

5 BEST PIECES OF ADVICE YOU HAVE EVER *been given*

1

2

3

4

5

5 WORST PIECES OF ADVICE YOU HAVE *been given*

1

2

3

4

5

5 CELEBRITIES
TO FOLLOW ON TWITTER

- ....
- ....
- ....
- ....
- ....

5 CELEBRITIES WHO SHOULDN'T BE ALLOWED to have Instagram accounts

1. ....
2. ....
3. ....
4. ....
5. ....

5 biggest LIES YOU'VE EVER TOLD

1

2

3

4

5

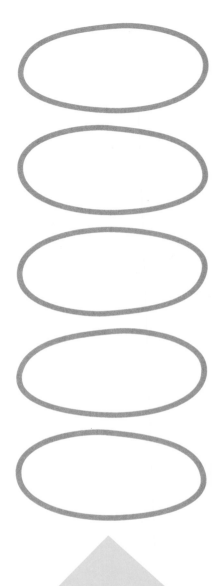

5 STUPIDEST THINGS you've ever BELIEVED

5 MOST *likely* CONSPIRACY THEORIES

1

2

3

4

5

5 THINGS THAT YOU *hope* ARE TRUE

1

2

3

4

5

5 PEOPLE WHOSE OPINIONS YOU VALUE

1

2

3

4

5

5 PEOPLE WHOSE ACTIONS YOU ADMIRE

1

2

3

4

5

5 THINGS YOU WOULD SAVE FROM A HOUSE FIRE

1

2

3

4

5

1

2

3

4

5

5 THINGS YOU WOULD HAPPILY LIVE WITHOUT

5 CELEBRITIES

YOU'D CROSS THE ROAD TO MEET

1 ....

2 ....

3 ....

4 ....

5 ....

5

CELEBRITIES YOU'D CROSS THE ROAD TO AVOID

1 ______________________

2 ______________________

3 ______________________

4 ______________________

5 ______________________

5 CELEBRITIES YOU WOULDN'T TRUST

1 ....

2 ....

3 ....

4 ....

5 ....

5 CELEBRITIES WHO WOULD GIVE GOOD ADVICE

1 ------------------------

2 ------------------------

3 ------------------------

4 ------------------------

5 ------------------------

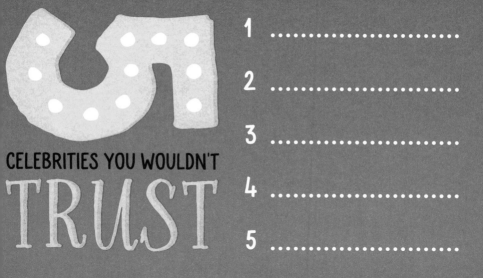

5 *best* OLD-SCHOOL HOBBIES

1

2

3

4

5

5 *most* POINTLESS HOBBIES

1

2

3

4

5

5 HOUSE RULES EVERYONE SHOULD FOLLOW

-
-
-
-
-

5 GYM RULES EVERYONE SHOULD FOLLOW

-
-
-
-
-

5 FASHIONS *that should be* REVIVED

1 ____________________

2 ____________________

3 ____________________

4 ____________________

5 ____________________

5 FASHIONS THAT SHOULD NEVER COME BACK

1

2

3

4

5

5

THINGS IN YOUR CLOSET YOU'LL NEVER THROW OUT

-
-
-
-
-

5 THINGS YOU'D WEAR *if you* DIDN'T CARE

1.
2.
3.
4.
5.

5 dream JOBS

1

2

3

4

5

5 DREAM JOB LOCATIONS

5 THINGS that make a GREAT BOSS

1

2

3

4

5

5 THINGS YOU WOULD *never* DO FOR A PROMOTION

1

2

3

4

5

5 SONGS THAT GO ON FOR TOO LONG

1

2

3

4

5

5 BEST THINGS TO DO WITH A SPARE 5 MINUTES

1

2

3

4

5

5 BEST
CHILDHOOD TOYS

1

2

3

4

5

1

2

3

4

5

5 BEST
CHILDHOOD TV SHOWS

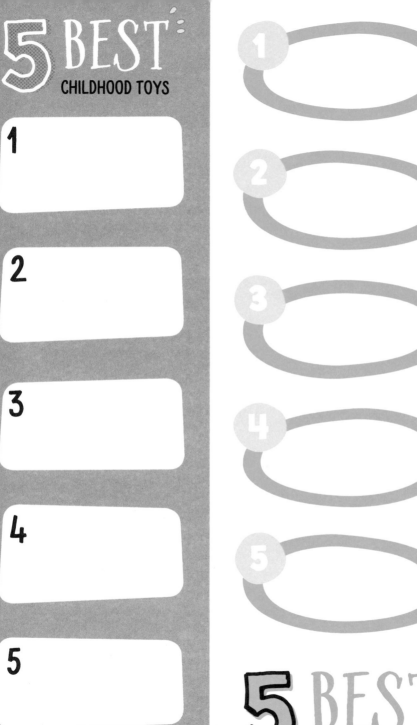

5 CELEBRITY COUPLES

WHO NEVER HAVE BEEN BUT SHOULD BE

1 ....

2 ....

3 ....

4 ....

5 ....

5 CELEBRITIES WHO MADE THE WRONG CAREER CHOICE

1 ______________________

2 ______________________

3 ______________________

4 ______________________

5 ______________________

5 CELEBRITIES WITH MORE FAME THAN TALENT

1 ....

2 ....

3 ....

4 ....

5 ....

5 CELEBRITIES

WHO ARE UNDERRATED

1 ----------------------

2 ----------------------

3 ----------------------

4 ----------------------

5 ----------------------

5 things YOU WISH YOU'D INVENTED

1

2

3

4

5

1

2

3

4

5

5 inventions WAITING TO HAPPEN

5 TALENTS YOU HAVE NEVER DEVELOPED

-
-
-
-
-

5 TALENTS YOU MOST ADMIRE

-
-
-
-
-

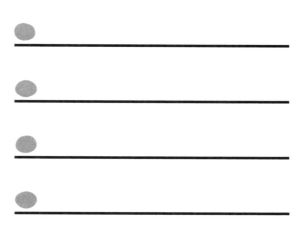

5 PEOPLE YOU WOULD *trust* WITH YOUR LIFE

1 ______

2 ______

3 ______

4 ______

5 ______

5 PEOPLE YOU'D SWAP PLACES WITH *for a week*

1

2

3

4

5

5 PUBLIC FIGURES YOU TRUST

-
-
-
-
-

5 LOST FRIENDS you'd like to be REUNITED WITH

1.
2.
3.
4.
5.

5 best PARTIES YOU HAVE BEEN TO

1

2

3

4

5

5 CELEBRATION DAYS you would CREATE

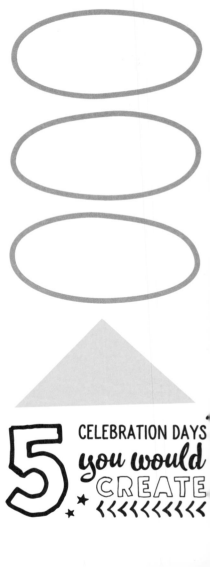

5 BEST GIFTS YOU HAVE EVER been given

1

2

3

4

5

5 gifts YOU'VE REGIFTED

1

2

3

4

5

5 BEST THINGS TO DO IN THE SUMMERTIME

1

2

3

4

5

5 VACATIONS THAT ARE BETTER THAN camping

1

2

3

4

5

5 BEST
WAYS TO TRAVEL

1

2

3

4

5

1

2

3

4

5

5 THINGS YOU ALWAYS PACK

5 GREAT THINGS

THAT COME IN SMALL PACKAGES

1 ....

2 ....

3 ....

4 ....

5 ....

5

WAYS TO SAY THANK-YOU

1 ______________________

2 ______________________

3 ______________________

4 ______________________

5 ______________________

5 PEOPLE YOU WILL NEVER FORGET

1 ....

2 ....

3 ....

4 ....

5 ....

5 DAYS YOU WILL NEVER FORGET

1 ---------------------------

2 ---------------------------

3 ---------------------------

4 ---------------------------

5 ---------------------------

5 GREATEST EVENTS in the history of the WORLD

5 most OVERRATED TV SHOWS

5

5 BANDS THAT SHOULD NEVER REUNITE

5 TV SHOWS YOU WOULD CANCEL

5 most UNPLEASANT PEOPLE YOU HAVE EVER MET

5 MOST DESTRUCTIVE inventions OF THE LAST 200 YEARS

5 WEBSITES YOU COULDN'T LIVE WITHOUT

5 GREATEST VLOGGERS

5 THINGS THAT KEEP YOU AWAKE

5 REASONS TO GO OUT

5 BOOKS YOU FEEL YOU SHOULD READ but probably never will

5 THINGS PEOPLE OVER 30 SHOULD never wear

5

5 CITIES YOU'D LIKE TO LIVE IN

5 THINGS THAT MAKE YOUR DAY

5 HOT MEALS THAT taste BETTER COLD

5 WIN awards YOU'D LIKE TO

5 THINGS THAT FREAK YOU OUT ON VACATION

5 THINGS THAT freak you out at HOME